Henry M. Nixdorff

Life of Whittier's Heroine Barbara Fritchie

Henry M. Nixdorff

Life of Whittier's Heroine Barbara Fritchie

ISBN/EAN: 9783337195861

Printed in Europe, USA, Canada, Australia, Japan

Cover: Foto ©Andreas Hilbeck / pixelio.de

More available books at **www.hansebooks.com**

LIFE OF

WHITTIER'S HEROINE,

BARBARA FRITCHIE;

INCLUDING A

BRIEF BUT COMPREHENSIVE SKETCH

—OF—

HISTORIC "OLD FREDERICK,"

BY HENRY M. NIXDORFF.

FREDERICK, MD.

W. T. DELAPLAINE & CO., PUBLISHERS AND PRINTERS.

1887.

JOHN G. WHITTIER.

BARBARA FRITCHIE.

Barbara Fritchie.

BY JOHN G. WHITTIER.

Up from the meadows rich with corn,
Clear in the cool September morn,

The clustered spires of Frederick stand
Green-walled by the hills of Maryland.

Round about them orchards sweep,
Apple and peach-tree fruited deep,

Fair as a garden of the Lord
To the eyes of the famished rebel horde,

On that pleasant morn of the early Fall
When Lee marched over the mountain-wall, —

Over the mountains winding down,
Horse and foot, into Frederick town.

Forty flags with their silver stars,
Forty flags with their crimson bars,

Flapped in the morning wind: the sun
Of noon looked down, and saw not one.

Up rose old Barbara Fritchie then,
Bowed with her fourscore years and ten;

Bravest of all in Frederick town,
She took up the flag the men hauled down;

In her attic-window the staff she set,
To show that one heart was loyal yet.

Up the street came the rebel tread,
Stonewall Jackson riding ahead.

Under his slouched hat left and right
He glanced; the old flag met his sight.

"Halt!"—the dust-brown ranks stood fast,
"Fire!"—out blazed the rifle-blast.

It shivered the window, pane and sash;
It rent the banner with seam and gash.

Quick, as it fell, from the broken staff
Dame Barbara snatched the silken scarf;

She leaned far out on the window-sill,
And shook it forth with a royal will.

"Shoot, if you must, this old gray head,
But spare your country's flag," she said.

A shade of sadness, a blush of shame,
Over the face of the leader came;

The nobler nature within him stirred
To life at that woman's deed and word;

"Who touches a hair of yon gray head
Dies like a dog! March on!" he said.

All day long through Frederick street
Sounded the tread of marching feet;

All day long that free flag tost
Over the heads of the rebel host.

Ever its torn folds rose and fell
On the loyal winds that loved it well;

And through the hill-gaps sunset light
Shone over it a warm good-night.

Barbara Fritchie's work is o'er,
And the Rebel rides on his raids no more.

Honor to her! and let a tear
Fall, for her sake, on Stonewall's bier.

Over Barbara Fritchie's grave
Flag of Freedom and Union, wave!

Peace and order and beauty draw
Round thy symbol of light and law;

And ever the stars above look down
On thy stars below in Frederick town!

PREFACE.

AS much that is utterly false has been published concerning my friend and neighbor, Mrs. Barbara Fritchie, since the appearance of the wonderful poem entitled "Barbara Fritchie", by that great and justly distinguished poet John G. Whittier, I deem it a duty, as one who loved her, for the many excellent traits of character that she possessed, as well as having been for many years her friend and well acquainted with her for a long time, to tell the public what I know of this worthy lady. The object I have in view, is not to produce anything sensational, or to distort, but to be careful, on the contrary, to make no statement that does not rest on a sure foundation, and I wish it understood that I shall give the exact truth in what I state in the following pages.

The German spelling of Fritchie would be "Freitchie," but we give the English as it was spelled on his small sign at the window where he was conducting business, "Fritchie."

LIFE OF

WHITTIER'S HEROINE,

"BARBARA FRITCHIE."

—>←—

MRS. SOUTHWORTH, the distinguished authoress, who was in Washington at the time, was the person who wrote to the poet concerning this estimable lady and enclosed a newspaper slip relating to Barbara Fritchie's action, when Gen. Lee's Army entered Frederick, and this led to the preparation by the poet of that wonderful poem.

Miss Barbara Hauer, was born in the flourishing city of Lancaster, Pennsylvania, December 3rd, 1766, and was baptized by the Rev. William Hendel, pastor of the Reformed Church, December 14th, 1766. Her parents names are recorded in the records of the First

Reformed Church of Lancaster City, as Nico-
las and Catherine Hauer. The names of their
five children were Daniel, George, Barbara,
Margaret and Catherine. After marriage they
were Mrs. John C. Fritchie, Mrs. Stover and
Mrs. Peter Mantz. Her husband had received
the military title of major and was well
known as Major Peter Mantz.

Attention is called at this point for a few
moments to Mr. John C. Fritchie the much
esteemed husband of our heroine. He was a
highly respected citizen of Frederick. His
humble and unobtrusive manner won for him
the regard of his fellow-citizens, and such is
ever the case. True merit is retiring and
unassuming.

He conducted a glove manufactory in the
East front room of his dwelling, and also pre-
pared the material in his shop fronting on
Carroll Creek.

His assistant in the glove department
was Mr. Henry Hanshew, who had married
Mrs. Fritchie's niece, an honorable man,
against whom nothing of evil could be justly
spoken.

I have frequently seen these two most excellent men early in the morning wending
their way to the city spring, to take a refresh-
ing draught of pure cold water, and afterward

with clean towels in hand, go to an outlet of the spring, and bathe hands and face, so as to feel its delightful effects before entering upon the regular duties of the day.

Mr. Fritchie was successful in business. While he did not acquire great wealth, he accumulated sufficient to live comfortably during life, and at his death, leave to his beloved wife the dwelling in which they had so long resided and means otherwise invested. His death occured Nov. 10th, 1849. Gone but not forgotten, for beautiful myrtle yet covers his grave.

Miss Barbara Hauer was born in exciting times, when the Colonies of America were still subject to England and stirring events were constantly transpiring.

Just previous to her birth the odious "stamp act", ordering that all papers on which instruments of writing were prepared should be taxed, at exorbitant rates, had been repealed and shortly after, May 1767, a second plan for taxing the colonists was adopted, while yet they were without representation in Parliament. This led to the preparation of that matchless paper "The Declaration of Independence", where each pledged his life, his honor and his fortune, in furtherance of this glorious cause.

The Declaration of Independence and asserting our freedom from British rule, was adopted some ten years after the birth of Miss Barbara Hauer. She was therefore one of those people of hardy orgin, who dared to do or die. She no doubt soon learned of the action taken by the citizens of Frederick-town, Maryland, in opposition to British oppression.

As early as 1765 in the old court house in Frederick was the obnoxious "stamp act" pronounced inoperative. And as early in the struggle for our right as 1775, when the battles of Lexington and Bunker Hill aroused the colonies to the succor of Massachusetts, two companies marched from Frederick-town for camp at Boston.

Our heroine was well informed in regard to, and quite conversant, with many events that transpired during the Revolutionary war, and knew full well at how great a sacrifice our national liberty had been obtained. Wonder not then that she stood firm as a rock in defense of her beloved country's best interests, now asserting its just rights.

By a long life of honesty and industry, Mrs. Fritchie enjoyed an honorable and enviable position in society. Therefore if defamer or wicked persons speak ought against her it will only cause her character to shine forth with more resplendent lustre.

BARBARA FRITCHIE'S HOUSE.

Patrick street in Frederick City is one of the principal streets, and extends East and West. Mrs. Fritchie's residence was on West Patrick street. It was built of brick and very substantial. It was not large, but neat; one story and a half in height, with two front doors, and three windows in front, beside two dormer windows on the roof. It was painted red and penciled in white, and the shutters were never painted other than pure white. Her home will easily be recognized on the illustrated page, which shows also Carroll creek and the adjoining buildings. The dormer window was at that time quite in style, now they are scarcely seen. Houses that were considered neat and beautiful years ago, are now thought to be quite ordinary.

At one of those dormer windows, I have frequently noticed her standing with her country's flag floating gracefully and beautifully from the same window.

In the early days of the rebellion, when one disaster after another had befallen the Union army, and other patriotic hearts were almost overwhelmed with grief and beginning to despond; when matters looked so dark, so portentious, she stood entirely unmoved, displaying the greatest composure imaginable. Her loyalty to the country of her birth was

of the most pronounced character. She never
suffered that country to be spoken of in her
presence in a disparaging way, without at
once, and in the most earnest manner, resent-
ing it. Yes, those small bright eyes would
flash with excitement and indignation and her
usual calmness, change to that of resolute-
ness and strong determination, until the of-
fensive remark was recalled, which was invariably done, for all knew that she meant what
she said in her inmost soul. She realized
that in "Union their is Strength," and believed
it with her whole heart.

I shall never forget her appearance as she
came into my store during the earlier part of
the war, leaning on her staff and saying with
the greatest earnestness, "do not for a moment
despair, stand firm."

Often when she entered the store, she
would ask, "how do matters look now for the
Union side?" Sometimes I had just heard
good news of a cheering character, and when
I would communicate it to her, joy was manifested in the most fervent manner. Her whole
frame kindled with emotion and her bright
eyes sparkled with delight. At other times
news of a saddening character had been received, and when I made it known to her I
felt greatly depressed. She would notice it at

once and remark, "O, do not be cast down, it will all come right, I know it will, the Union must be preserved," and remark with the greatest emphasis, "Be assured that God takes care of his people, and he will take care of this country. I feel perfectly satisfied that the Union of the States will be maintained. I am sure that it is God's will that the Union shall continue and you know that nothing can stand against that." Thus it was that encouragement was given by this patriotic lady when many strong men became lukewarm and indifferent, and even when the Flag of the land that gave them birth was ruthlessly assailed. Although more than twenty years have elapsed since that time, yet that aged form, that feeble step, I never can, never shall forget. She was one of those persons who impress you favorably at the first interview, and that impression strengthens as time rolls on. I loved her, though aged and weak, and treasure up as precious, the words I heard her speak. If her Country did wrong she would not forsake, but endeavor to place her in the right. True, she had lived more than ninety years of pleasure, pain, toil, and tears, but it only made her attachment take deeper root for the cause of her Country, the cause of truth. Yes, she loved this blessed land of lands, upon which

Heaven has showered its richest blessings. She had great will power, and such persons accomplish most in this world, although in the political arena women can do but little, not having the right to express sentiments through the ballot box; yet by well directed efforts and influence in certain directions she has already accomplished much. Look, for instance, at what has been done by the Womans' Christian Temperance Union for the cause of humanity!

Mrs. Fritchie was not robust, but decision of character was seen throughout, and judging from her eyes and mouth she surely was not one to be trifled with. If she said, No! it was quite plain that she was settled in the opinion formed, and to change it was no easy task, for when formed aright it was formed to last. In conversation she was quite refined, her language was always chaste, entirely pure; thus setting an example which was no doubt the means of leading many in the right direction. Persons calling on her were sure to meet with a kind, cordial welcome. Carroll Creek, a small stream, flowed past the gable-end of her back building on its way to the Monocacy. At one of the windows that looked out upon the creek I have frequently, on my way to the Spring, now known as "City Spring," noticed her sitt-

ing, either sewing, knitting, or reading some
favorite book, always busily engaged in doing
something. It is not to be wondered at, therefore, that she understood household duties, or
that she could converse intelligently upon almost any subject. As a wife she was thoroughly domestic and by her genial disposition and
well stored mind made home what it ever
should be—a happy, lovable and attractive
place. To so great an extent was this the case
that her beloved husband was seldom absent
from it when the evening shades gathered
around. Thus happy, thus joyous, could every
home be made.

She was the senior of her husband by a
number of years. I have frequently heard my
mother remark that a company of young ladies
were present at a quilting party, when it was
announced that a son had been born to Mrs.
Fritchie. Among the young ladies attending
the party was the beautiful and accomplished
Miss Barbara Hauer, who in the course of time
became the beloved and devoted wife of Mr.
John C. Fritchie whose birth it was that was
announced that night. I do not suppose that
our heroine ever weighed over 110 or 115
pounds. She was slight in figure and scarcely
of medium height, her eyes were small but
penetrating and keen, her hair was dark in

early life, but at last the silver threads began
to take the place of the dark brown. At length,
having lost much of her hair, she was induced
to purchase a braid, which gave her the appearance of one much younger than she really
was.   In her dress she was remarkable for
plainness, the variations were few   indeed.
About the house her costume was usually that
of plain quaker colored calico, and when she
went to the store, or when she visited neighbors or attended church, you could rest assured
that she would be clad in a black cashmere or
alapaca dress, though she had a handsome
plum colored silk and other costly dresses,
which she could have worn. She was a poor
visitor, seldom going among her neighbors,
and, all things considered, perhaps too much
visiting is not to be commended. She posess-
ed much beautiful chinaware. A relative of
her's residing in our City has at the present
time cups and saucers, tea pot and other chinaware, which formerly belonged to Mrs. Fritchie,
also gold ear rings and an excellent likeness
of her aged relative. Out of the tea pot Gen.
George Washington drank tea the night he
spent in Frederick, in the year 1791. The
way it happened was as follows: The young
ladies of the town had a quilting party at Mrs.
Kimball's Hotel, where the City Hotel is now

located. They entertained Gen. Washington, and Miss Barbara Hauer loaned her chinaware to grace the table. When Gen. Washington died these same young ladies held a sham funeral and our heroine acted as one of the pall bearers. She was not accustomed to speak in a boasting way of any act that she performed, for she considered that when in the discharge of duty she was only doing that which she believed to be right. Therefore she did not understand why a person should be so highly complimented for doing what God's word taught her was the right, and which if she deviated from would be taking a step in the wrong direction. The poor and distressed ever had a sympathising friend in her, and though not able to do or give as much as some others, she did all she could. This is all that is required, for you know it is said in God's blessed word, that if we only give a cup of cold water with the proper spirit to one in need it is pleasing in the sight of our Heavenly Father.

She was benevolent, in the highest sense of the term, not making excuses, as some do, and turning worthy and unworthy persons indiscriminately from her door. I feel assured that plain, unostentacious benevolence is such as is acceptable in Jehovah's sight. She never courted the society of the great and noble of the

earth, if pride and wealth alone made them such
in the sight of those with whom they associated.
She was fond of cultivating flowers.   Between
the front house and the back building at her
residence there was a small triangular parcel
of ground.   This she had planted with beautiful flowers and very often you might find
her at work in this little flower garden.   I re-
member as clearly as though it were but yes-
terday of frequently standing on the bridge
adjoining and viewing the lovely roses, dahl-
ias, chrysanthemums, as well as other flowers
blooming in this little bed.   I cannot forget
that they appeared to me to be unusually
pretty, accounted for I suppose from the fact
that being near the creek the ground was
constantly moist.   The pink rose trained
against the wall was always nicely trimmed,
and during Summer and Autumn was rarely
other than in full bloom.   Our heroine was of
a cheerful disposition.   Persons not acquainted with her would not have supposed that such
was the case, for many persons when advanced
in years, if the least feeble or infirm, become
cross and disagreeable.   It was not so with
her.   She enjoyed anything of an amusing
nature very much indeed and would partici-
pate in the conversation of young people with
much pleasure.   She never feared to do or say

when she felt that God directed her steps. Leaning on the "Rock of Ages" she needed no other support. For a sure stronghold is our God to all that put their trust in him.

Mrs. Fritchie had never been blessed with children. Miss Yoner, a relative, lived with her for a number of years and was a great comfort, especially when she became somewhat enfeebled by age. In speaking of the brave volunteer going forth in defense of his home and the land of his birth, our heroine said to me, that if she had been blest with children she would cheerfully have given her sons to the service of this great country. Yes, dearly as she would have loved them, she would have thought no sacrifice too great.

The volunteer or private soldier, is the pride and strong defense of this country, for here we keep no large standing armies supported by the Government to protect us. Previous to her death, after many battles had been fought and won on the side of the Union, she said to me one day, "You know how often I assured you that thus it would be, and now see how my words are being verified."

The Confederate soldiers, in the most destitute and forlorn condition, were those accompanying the command of General Jackson when his celebrated raid was made into Mary-

land and Frederick City. They were shoeless,
hatless, and, in fact, destitute and in want of
almost everything; begging for something to
eat, for even if they had Confederate money
they could not in most instances pass it. I
shall never forget their appearance. I was
engaged in connection with another gentleman
in the dry goods trade in Frederick City, and
of course we had to bear considerable loss.
Having a large country trade, we kept besides
the regular goods, boots, shoes, hats and caps.
I do not think that I shall ever forget how I
felt when three Confederate soldiers came into
the store and asked me,—when I was alone—
to show them some shoes and then asked the
price. They were the first Southern soldiers
I had met or seen. I handed the shoes down
from the shelves. Two pair were each priced
$1.50, the othe pair $1.75. They said, "We
will take the three pair." I wrapped them up,
when one of the soldiers handed me a $20.00
Confederate note and waited for the change.
You can easily imagine the dilemma I was in.
I would not give him change in United States
money, and therefore gave him the note back,
which amused them all very much. They
picked up the package of shoes and went out
and away. I looked around and saw that the
store was getting crowded with soldiers, in

front, back of the counter and everywhere. Of course one or two of us could do nothing. If we could have waited on them they would have been willing to pay with such money as they had, and some of them did hand a ten or twenty dollar Confederate note and took shoes, boots and hats to the full amount. The majority, however, would throw the boots and shoes across their arms and move off without saying a word, even my own hat and boots kept for occasional wear were taken. When the Confederate army, led by Generals Lee, Jackson and others, entered Frederick City, on Saturday morning, September 6, 1862, it is said that as they came marching up East Patrick street Gen. Jackson was in command, at least for some time. It is certain that their appearance did not occasion the uprising of the people that the Confederate Generals had been led to expect from a people who were thought to be down-trodden and oppressed. Many of hose, even, who were thought to be in sympathy with them did not open their doors to welcome them. On Monday, September 8th, Gen. Lee issued his proclamation to the people of Maryland calling on them to throw off the restraint of the Union Government and join the South. A general uprising of the people was no doubt expected to result from

the invitation, which, however, did not receive
the slightest response. The following is the
proclamation:

HEADQUARTERS ARMY N. VA., }
Near Frederick Town, Sept. 8, 1862. }

TO THE PEOPLE OF MARYLAND: ·

It is right that you should know the purpose that has brought the army under my
command within the limits of your State, so
far as that purpose concerns yourselves.

The people of the Confederate States have
long watched with the deepest sympathy the
wrongs and outrages that have been inflicted
upon the citizens of a Commonwealth allied to
the States of the South be the strongest social,
political and commercial ties.

They have seen with profound indignation their sister State deprived of every right
and reduced to the condition of a conquered
province.

Under the pretense of supporting the
Constitution, but in violation of its most valu-
able provisions, your citizens have been arrest-
ed and imprisoned upon no charge and contrary to all forms of law; the faithful and
manly protest against this outrage, made by
the venerable and illustrious Marylander to
whom in better days no citizen appealed for
right in vain, was treated with scorn and con-
tempt. The government of your city has
been usurped by armed strangers; your Leg-
lature been dissolved by the unlawful arrest
of its members; freedom of the press and

speech have been suppressed ; words have been declared offenses by an arbitrary decree of the Federal executive and citizens ordered to be tried by a military commission for what they may dare to speak. Believing that the people of Maryland possessed a spirit too lofty to submit to such a government, the people of the South have long wished to aid you in throwing off this foreign yoke, to enable you to again enjoy the inalienable rights of freemen and restore independency and sovereignty to your State.

In obedience to this wish our army has come among you and is prepared to assist you with the power of its arms in regaining the rights of which you have been dispoiled.

This, citizens of Maryland, is our mission, so far as yourselves are concerned. No restraint upon your free will is intended; no intimidation will be allowed within the limits of this army, at least Marylanders shall once more enjoy their ancient freedom of thought and speech.

We know of no enemies among you, and will protect all of every opinion. It is for you to decide your destiny, freely and without restraint.

This army will respect your choice whatever it may be, and while the Southern people will rejoice to welcome you to your natural position among them, they will only welcome you when you come of your own free will.

R. E. LEE, Commanding.

To General Lee's great surprise his proclamation created no enthusiasm whatever, but
fell entirely harmless, gaining nothing in the
way of aid or comfort, but on the contrary in-
tensifying the feeling of loyalty and devotion
to the Union. In the language of Col. J.
Thomas Scharf in his history of Western
Maryland, "The reception of the Confederate
troops, by the inhabitants of Frederick, was
decidedly cool. Not the slightest mani-
festation of joy and enthusiasm was exhibited.
With all places of business closed and the
streets deserted by the people, the old town
wore a gloomy appearance in striking contrast
to the resplendency displayed, upon the entry
of the Union army one week later."

On Wednesday morning, Sept. 10th, 1862,
the Confederate army began to move out of
Frederick city.

General Jackson's corps was in the advance. As they passed out West Patrick street,
I stood at the front window of my dwelling
looking at regiment after regiment, clad in
grey or brown uniforms, as they marched past
for several hours. So intent was I in noticing
and reflecting on this lamentable action on the
part of the people against the best government
on earth that I lost sight of what was going on
at Mrs. Fritchie's, although her residence was

not a square distant from my own. But this I do
believe, that if the opportunity was presented
she did not fail to improve it, for I do not
think that she would have taken a backward
step though confronted by their entire army.
In the language of Mrs. Abbott, "Aunt
Fritchie was fearless and very patriotic." A
single incident will show the spirit animating
her. On one occasion a number of Confederate soldiers halted and sat down on the porch
in front of her dwelling, and were drinking
water brought from the spring near by. To
this she had not the least objection, but before
leaving they began to speak in a derogatory
manner of her beloved country. In a moment
she arose and passing to the front door she
bade them clear themselves and applied the
"cane," with which she used to walk, in the
most vigorous manner, clearing the porch in a
few moments of every man upon it. I am in-
clined to believe from enquiry that General
Jackson on the day the Confederates passed
through Frederick, did not pass by the dwelling of Mrs. Fritchie. It appears that he left
his soldiers, at the East end of the city, to call
on the Rev. Dr. John B. Ross, pastor of the
Presbyterian church, the wife of whom was the
daughter of Ex-Gov. McDowell, of Virginia,
with whom he was well acquainted. It being

early in the morning it is declared that he wrote the following note, and slipped it under the front door at Dr. Ross's dwelling.

REV. JOHN B. ROSS:—

Regret not being able to see you and Mrs. Ross, but could not expect to have that pleasure at so unseasonable an hour,

T. J. JACKSON.

Dr. Ross resided on West Second street, and it is stated that Gen. Jackson on leaving Dr. Ross's residence rode on to what is known as Bentz street and rejoined his soldiers by coming up a portion of Bentz street, commonly called "Mill Alley," which leads out into Patrick street a short distance beyond or on the West side of Mrs. Fritchie's residence. I measured the distance from "Mill Alley" to her dwelling and found it 63 yards. Grant that it was not Gen. Jackson, might it not have been some other officer in command, if so it would not change the principle involved. I have, however, no personal knowledge of its occurrence. This I do know; called for a moment to my front door that morning to see a friend, I happened to look up the street, and saw a very intelligent lady, a neighbor, standing on her front porch, with a small United States flag in her hand waving it and making apparently the most earnest remarks to a Con-

WEST PATRICK STREET, LOOKING SOUTH.

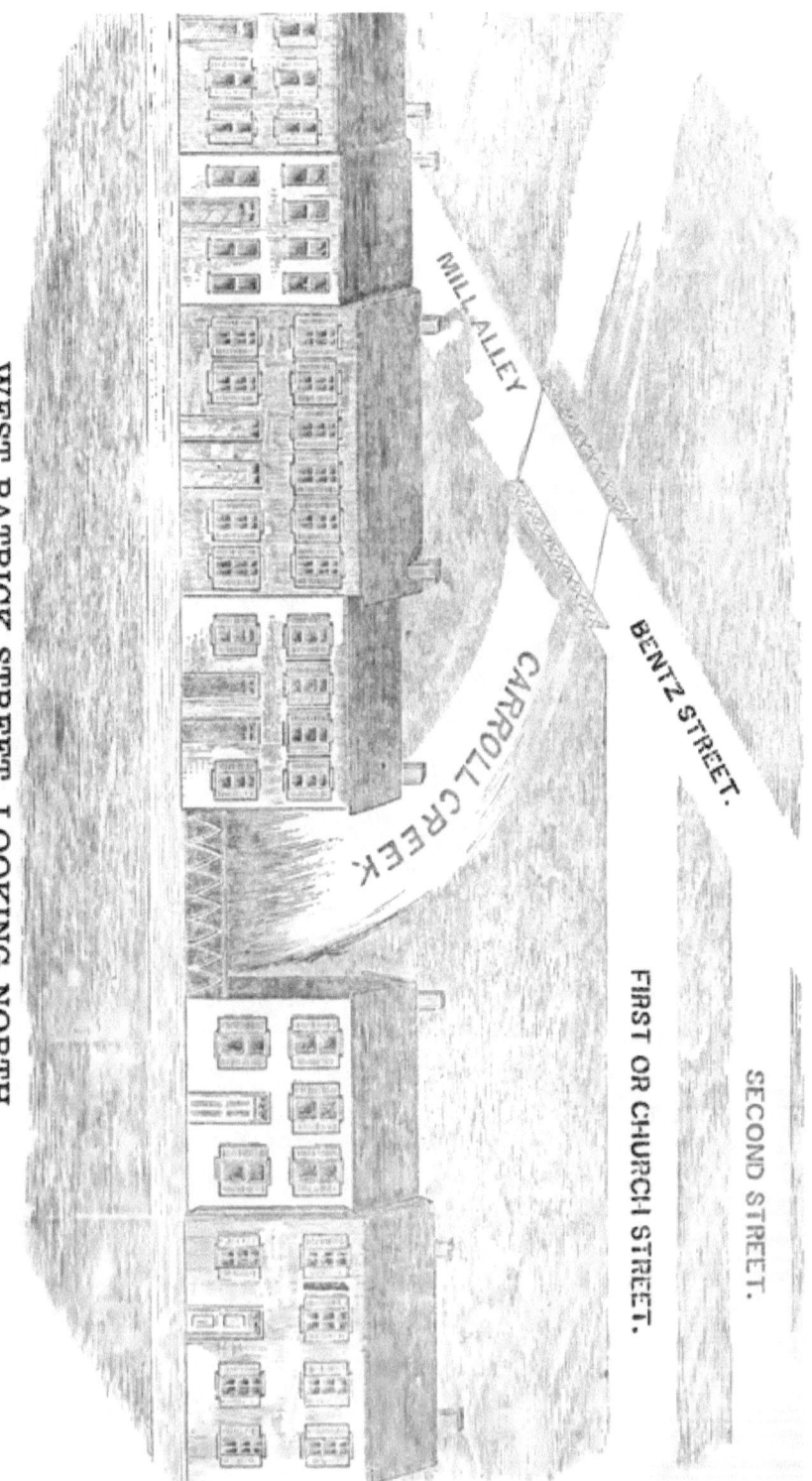

WEST PATRICK STREET, LOOKING NORTH.

MILL ALLEY

BENTZ STREET.

CARROLL CREEK

FIRST OR CHURCH STREET.

SECOND STREET.

federate officer who had ridden his horse over
on the pavement up to the porch where she
was standing. I was afterward assured by
those who had the pleasure of being present
that such glowing words of patriotism fell from
the lips of Mrs. Quantrell that the officer
looked on, and listened with wonder and surprise, and whilst he was present would not allow his men do her the least harm. After his
departure, however some of the soldiers belonging to the army came and knocked the
flag from her hand, breaking the staff into
several pieces.

In order to corroborate what I had written
I addressed the following note to Mr. Fleming,
and all his brothers and sisters joined in at-
testing to its correctiveness.

MR. WILLIAM W. FLEMING:—

Esteemed friend, will you please give me
the information that I desire if it is in your
power to do so. When some years since the
Confederate army passed through Frederick
city, it is said that your neighbor at that time,
Mrs. Mary Quantrell, stood on the porch in
front of her house and waved a small United
States flag, and that a Confederate officer rode
up to the porch and remonstrated with her for
doing so and urged her to desist, whereupon
she spoke to him in such glowing words of
patriotism that he was quite astonished, listen-

ed to her most respectfully, and whilst he was present would not allow her to be disturbed; that after his departure soldiers belonging to the army came up and knocked the flag out of her hand several times, breaking the flag staff. Is the foregoing correct? By answering the questions propounded you will greatly oblige   Your friend,

H. M. NIXDORFF.

We the undersigned find the foregoing statement to be correct.

Mrs. Matilda Fleming,
Mrs. Hallie M. McDonald,
Mrs. Kate H. Cashour,
Nicholas H. Fleming,
Wm. W. Fleming.

If this occured at Mrs. Mary Quantrell's we should not be astonished at anything said to have taken place at any other point.

On the 12th of September Gen. McClellan's army entered Frederick city. The advance was under command of Gen. Burnside. As they moved up West Patrick street on the National pike leading westward, they passed Mrs. Fritchie's residence. She was standing at one of the front windows of her dwelling, leaning on her cane. Beside her stood her relative, Miss Julia Hanshew, now Mrs. John N. Abbott; and Miss Yoner. As she stood by the window she waved her hand time and again to express her joy. Miss Yoner, no doubt at Mrs. Fritchie's request, went into the adjoining room and brought forth Mrs. Fritchie's flag. The old lady grasped it and stood at the window waving it. As she waved her flag the soldiers were perfectly delighted, some of them loudly cheering her, others ran to the window and as soon as they could get near enough grasped her by the hand and said "God bless you old lady, may you live long you dear old soul." And then cheer after cheer was given as our noble soldiers marched along. That same silk flag I have had in my hands only a short time since. Among those who shook hands with her that day was the beloved and valiant Gen. Reno.

It has been said truthfully, that the sun never shone upon a more patriotic people during those trying times, than the loyal Union men and women of the South, of which type our heroine was a distinguished example. She had early secured a United States flag, and often during the earlier part of the rebellion when matters looked dark and threatening to the Union army, I have seen that glorious emblem of our country's honor floating from the dormer window of her house, and my old neighbor standing beside the flag-staff looking intently at that which is the symbol of freedom, equality before the law, and the just rights of mankind wherever unfurled. A consecrated, blessed emblem. Thousands upon thousands have laid down their lives in its defense, and if required in the future, myriads would step forth to do the same thing, willing to die that the old flag might still wave.

Three miles south-east of Frederick City the battle of the Monocacy River was fought. The Union soldiers were of Gen. Tyler's division and under command of Gen. Lewis Wallace. They fought valiently but were finally repulsed by the enemy, who were in superior numbers, after many had been slain and wounded on both sides. As the Union army withdrew they set fire to and burned the large wooden bridge spanning the Monocacy at this point, so that the Confederates, who were on the western bank of the river, found it more difficult to pursue them. Some seventeen miles westward from Frederick City the battle of South Mountain was fought, September 14, 1862. It was a battle of great interest and magnitude. The excitement in Frederick was almost unbounded, for it looked as though our beloved State of Maryland might become the central battle ground between the North and the South, and our citizens be called upon to witness terrible scenes. Happily, this was averted, but many of our people nevertheless suffered severely by having their property taken from them at different periods, particularly by the raids of the enemy. As General McClellan's army or division was moving on the National pike, leading westward, they had several skirmishes with the enemy. The one on Catoctin mountain was quite severe, lasting however, only a short time. The discharge of the musketry could be heard distinctly in Frederick. The battle of South Mountain was a decided victory for the Union side. It was with saddened hearts, however, that we learned that in the engagement the brave and noble Gen. Reno, who only a few days previous had grasped the venerable Mrs. Fritchie by the hand, lost his life whilst worthily discharging his duty.

As I have said much in favor of our aged heroine, you might possibly suppose that I regarded her as perfect. Now this would be an incorrect conclusion, for I am well aware that we have had but one perfect character in this sin-cursed world, and that was our blessed Lord and Saviour. We do say, however, that if faults and blemishes did exist—and we do not for a moment doubt it—they were unknow to the writer of these pages. It may be

that her many virtues and excellencies so completely overshadowed her faults as to render
them undiscoverable to those by whom she
was surrounded. I was conversing recently
with Mr. John Riehl, a neighbor of mine for
many years, and with whom I have been in-
timately acquainted. He was also for many
years a neighbor of Mrs. Fritchie's. Speaking
of our heroine, he said, that when a boy he
was sent to Mrs. Fritchie's every day for milk,
for she kept a cow for many years. Said Mr.
Riehl: "You know the old lady had a decided
way of speaking." I said, "Yes." "Well,"
continued Mr. Riehl, "Sometimes when I
would reach her house the milking had not
been completed and she would say to me, 'Take
that small branch from the tree and keep the
flies from disturbing the cow whilst being
milked.' I quickly did as commanded but
always kept an eye on her, fearing that she
might give me a whipping if I did not do it to
please her. After I reached manhood and met
her often I found that she possessed one of the
kindest hearts imaginable."

During the days of slavery, long before
the war, Mr. and Mrs. Fritchie were the owners of slaves. "Fritchie's Harry" and "Aunt
Nellie" were known quite well. "Harry"
used to work in the skin dressing department

and "Old Aunt Nellie," at the household duties. They were very clever people, and were treated with great kindness by their owners. They in turn, loved "Old Massa" and "Old Missus," insomuch that when Harry was allowed to go and do for himself and live in another part of the town he would be constantly coming back to see "Old Massa" and "Old Missus" up to the time of his death. If the same kind feeling had existed between all owners of slaves, several of the most thrilling chapters in "Uncle Tom's Cabin," by Mrs. Stowe, would never have been written in truth.

You will pardon, I feel assured, a digression before proceeding further with the life of our heroine, by calling attention briefly to another remarkable person, a native of Frederick county.

About thirteen miles to the north-west of Frederick City, is located the former residence of that intelligent christian hero, George Blessing. He lived his lifetime in Middletown Valley, and bore an irreproachable character. He was known for a considerable distance around for his deeds of valor and heroism. I will give a short account of this distinguished patriot. His library did not consist of a choice collection, culled from the most distinguished authors of the day. No! it consisted of only a few books, but these were of the very best, and were read over and over again. He never became weary of perusing two of them; his well worn Bible, and the "Lives of American Statesmen." On his countenance firmness was depicted, and his broad forehead indicated sound judgment. His eyes were blue, and in his bosom beat a kind and noble heart. I have a photograph which is a perfect likeness of Mr. Blessing. The original was loaned me by one of his near relatives, who prizes it very highly. When the Confederate army came into Maryland, Mr. Blessing's home afforded temporary shelter for those fleeing before the advancing foe. On leaving they always advised him to accompany them, but he invariably refused, saying that he intended to remain and by God's help protect his home and family. I have been at his former home since the close of the war, and it is surely a beautiful and romantic place. When the battle of South Mountain was being fought the report of the artillery and discharge of the musketry could be distinctly heard at his residence known as "Highlands." He had on hand several old guns which he had obtained at different periods. These he commenced cleaning and loading, with the assistance of his son, Lewis. On the morning of the 9th of September, news came that the enemy was approaching the boundaries of his farm. His situation, considering how strong a Union man he had always been, was indeed perilous; but he was perfectly calm and asked his family to engage with him in prayer, in which he implored the Almighty to protect him and all the beloved members of his family, and if in accordance with His will still uphold the old flag. Such scenes make lasting impressions on those present. He listened not to the entreaties of the female portion of his family to still make his escape. Calling his son Lewis to take two of the guns, they started for the barn-yard, where they secreted themselves and awaited the approach of the foe. They soon saw a squad of men approaching. The invaders drew near cautiously, and not meeting with opposition one of them dismounted and commenced breaking open the stable door. Mr. Blessing called out in a loud voice, "If you touch that door again you shall surely suffer." They all looked around and gazed in every direction but were unable to determine from whence the sound came. They looked startled, as though they had heard an unearthly sound. At length they became calm and began their work again. Mr. Blessing and his son fired their guns at the same time upon the intruders. Both balls proved effective. The right arm dropped at the side of one of the men. The balance observing a cross-fire, and believing that a large force was hidden and waiting to be attacked, fled at once leaving their wounded comrade behind, and loudly declaring that they would return and take revenge on Mr. Blessing and his support- ers. As they were retreating Mr. Blessing fired a second shot after them. It entered the back of one of their number and he fell dead on the ground. Mr. Blessing took the man that was wounded to his own home and had his wounds dressed. As the old hero met his beloved wife he exclaimed, "Praise God, we are yet safe." His wife fearing that they might return in large numbers, once more urged him to seek refuge in flight, but he said he had abiding cofidence in the true and living God and therefore stood unmoved. He loaded his guns once more, and having given orders about the family not leaving the house, started for the stable. When he reached that point he helped to place the body of the dead man in the stable, subsequently it was buried, and then waited for the foe. He did not have to wait long, for soon a number of horsemen heavily armed came riding down the lane. When they had gotten near where Mr. Blessing was, three of the men

were ordered to go foreward and find out what
force the old hero had at his command with
which to oppose them, and return as soon as
possible and report. As they were passing
the clump of trees, Mr. Blessing shouted
"halt!" and then said, "what is your business?"
They replied, "to learn what force you have."
Then said Mr. Blessing, "form into line and
cross the road, and enter into my service, the
man disobeying will be instantly shot." They
did as commanded. The soldiers in the distance
fired vigorously at Mr. Blessing, and he just
as earnestly returned their fire. They knew
not what to do. At length, believing the old
hero's force to be much larger than it really
was, they concluded to withdraw. As they
wheeled around Mr. Blessing quickly aimed a
shot at the leader of the band and wounded
him severly, for he was seen to fall forward on
his horse's neck, and was hurriedly taken
away by his fellow soldiers. The men whom
he had captured stood almost dumbfounded at
what they had witnessed. On dismissing them
he gave each man his hand, and urged one
and all of them in the most heartfelt manner
to be true in the future to God and his country. When he reached home, it is impossible
to express the joy of his beloved family at re-
ceiving him once more. If they shed tears,

if they threw their arms around and embraced
him, we need not wonder, for his was almost a
miraculous preservation. "Blessed be God,"
he said, "for he has protected and defended
me." A third time he reloaded his gun and
walked down the lane. It was not long before
a large force was seen approaching. Resolv-
ing to die, if die he must, with his face to the
foe, he came out away from all concealment,
and raising his gun, was making ready to fire,
when he noticed a white flag waving. What
can it mean he thought. It surely must be
the sign for a truce. You can readily imagine
his joy at discovering as they drew near that
instead of enemies they were friends. Cole's
Cavalry, who were some distance off, learning
of his situation and bravery at once hastened
toward his residence to extend all the assistance in their power.

We must now resume the history of our
heroine. She enjoyed remarkably good health,
scarcely knowing what it was to be sick, until
the last and of course fatal attack came on,
when like a sheaf of wheat, ready to be garner-
ed, she gently and sweetly rested in the arms
of her Saviour. Having been clothed with
immortal life, she reached that city out of
sight whose builder and maker is God. Yes,
Mrs. Fritchie at length became enfeebled by

age and gathering her robes about her, she calmly waited for the coming of her blessed Lord. He came on that bleak, cold, 18th day of December 1862. All without was dreary and gloomy, but within that chamber of death there was perfect peace, beautifully exemplifying that passage of Scripture "Those shall rest in perfect peace whose minds are stayed on Him." Life's flickering lamp at length ceased to burn, and as far as this world is concerned all was over, all had closed. We doubt not but that our aged friend is now enjoying and will forever enjoy raptures of bliss around the throne of God. How precious is such a memory. Ninety some years to God and her country given, and now at home in Heaven. What a glorious thought it is, that after life's cares and anxieties are all over,—and some in passing through this world meet with so much trouble,—we reach at length the New Jerusalem, to go out no more forever. Mrs. Fritchie's remains rest in the Cemetery of the Reformed Church in Frederick City, in a lot enclosed with an iron railing, beside her husband. A neat block of marble has been placed at the head of the grave, and bears the following inscription.

"Barbara Fritchie, died December 18th, 1862. Aged 96 years."

Her age as given me by Mrs. Hanshew, taken from the old family Bible, was 96 years and 15 days. A small block of marble at the foot of the grave, bears the initials "B. F."

The block of marble at the head of her husband's grave is similar to that of his wife's, and reads:

"John C. Fritchie, died November 10th, 1849. Aged 69 years."

The small block at the foot bears the initials "J. C. F." The Cemetery is beautifully located, somewhat elevated toward the eastern part, or front, and gradually declining as it extends westward. It fronts on Bentz street, at the West end of Second street. On visiting the Cemetery lately I found a small United States flag gently waving over her grave. It needs no storied urn or animated bust to perpetuate her memory or that of Francis Scott Key, a Marylander by birth and a native of this county, whose remains have been deposited in Mount Olivet Cemetery in this city. And yet I hope that ere long monuments of an imposing character, will be erected to the memory of these distinguished patriots. Summer in all its beauty may come and go, wintry winds around us rudely blow, but who shall know the time when the youthful heart shall cease to glow at the mention of Barbara

Fritchie's name. O, how much from such an example we may learn! It gleams forth at almost every turn, and one of the leading facts that we should discern, is, that our hearts should ever burn with love and devotion to our blessed country. Any one can speak well of his country when all is calm and clear, when naught can do us harm. Who need fear, at such a time, even an Arnold may appear to hold his country's interest dear and speak in her defense. O where could baser ingratitude appear, than after enjoying our country's blessings far and near, she should call, and we turn a deaf ear, or be a stumbling block in the way.

May we to our country be firm as a rock or wall, willing for her to stand or fall, ready for her to risk our lives, our all. Such was Barbara Fritchie. Her brothers and sisters have long since passed from this sphere of action. All of them have exchanged time for eternity. Numerous relatives however, are still living. A son of Mr. Daniel Hauer, relatives of Mrs. Catherine Mantz, children of Mr. George Hauer and the widow of Mr. Henry Hanshew and her children, beside others distantly related, reside in our midst, and are among our very best and most useful citizens. Mr. George Eissler purchased the "Fritchie property," after the decease of our heroine from the heirs, and conducted the dyeing business at that place for several years. Whilst Mr. Eissler owned the property we were visited by the "great freshet" of July 24th, 1868. The water rose to a great height and washed out a corner of the "Fritchie building." Afterward the Corporation of Frederick, from a desire to avoid danger in the future, bought the property from Mr. Eissler and after selling the building as it stood, on the lot from which it was removed in a short time by Mr. James Hopwood the purchaser, the Corporation commenced the work of widening the stream, taking in a portion of the lot, where Mrs. Fritchie formerly resided, and subsequently sold the balance of the lot to Mr. James Hopwood, whose son, James W. Hopwood, purchased it from his father and erected a two-story brick dwelling with store room in front, where he has conducted the tinning business ever since. When the work of removing the building commenced the deep interest felt in our aged deceased neighbor was manifested by many of the citizens gathering around and collecting small bits of wood from doors and window frames. This continued until the gentleman who had purchased the material of the building, announced that he

would make a number of canes out of the wood
of the window frames and rafters, which were
of solid oak, and furnish them to the public at
a reasonable price. This he did, and some persons secured several, to present to valued
friends as "mementoes." Polished up nicely
they presented a very pretty appearance.
Meeting a friend with one on the street a short
time since I asked him what amount he would
take for it. "Oh," said he, "I would not take
anything in reason, for I do not know where
I could obtain another."

What could rejoice the heart of Mrs.
Fritchie more, who has long since reached the
"Everlasting City," than looking down from
her celestial home (for we believe that the
spirits in bliss are cognizant of what is going
on in this world,) upon the land she so much
loved, and seeing that land growing in wealth
and in power; taking her place among the
most notable nations on earth in rank and influence. Go on, our native land, may God
give us grace to sustain thy free institutions
and uphold thy laws. The government of the
United States is now acknowledged to be the
best on earth by all fair minded people, for
here all the officers are elected by and held
responsible to the people for all official acts.
The various nations of the earth are now treat-

ing with the greatest respect and consideration
the United States, observing that she is rapidly increasing in population and making great
progress each passing hour in science, art and
agricultural, and it will doubtless continue until we attain to the most complete develope-
ment possible.

Our territory is now reaching far and
wide, and we have no doubt, but that it is
destined some day to include Canada and
Cuba. The worthy emigrant can here se-
cure a home and become a citizen of this great
country. It is our duty to take such by the
hand and show them that by industry and
sobriety they may attain to high positions of
trust and influence, as well as respectability,
and enjoy the rights and privileges of freemen, such as were unknown to them in
the "Fatherland." But in order to become
such citizens they must endeavor to assimi-
late with our government and give their
cordial support to all the principles and
laws that have in the past conduced to
make us a great people. A most gratifying
fact to every lover of his country, is, that,
twenty-five years have worked wondrous
changes in the minds of the American people,
and many doctrines deemed false and unten-
able at that time are now accepted as truths

and acquiesced in by the great masses of the people of the United States. And we have the glorious knowledge that from North to South, and from East to West, all over this vast domain, where heretofore alienation existed, you now find a spirit of concord and brotherly love springing up, which is so essential to happiness and all that renders life enjoyable and enables us to bear patiently the difficulties with which we have to contend. It is a blessed thing to have peace in a family and also in the nation, doing entirely away with discord and strife and all ill-nature, especially such evil feelings as have been engendered by the warfare of one section of our beloved country against another. It has to be, however, a gradual work, for the great animosity, yea! genuine hatred, exhibited by one section toward the other can only be eradicated as time rolls on. It is a blessed thing to forgive and forget. We rejoice that the time is hastening on when brother and friend shall heartily greet each other and let the dead past be blotted out of rememberance from one portion of the country to the other. So that, with loving expressions, the Blue and the Grey, who had engaged in many a desperate conflict on the battle-field, where both displayed great bravery amid most trying scenes, where the courage of the one or the other was never questioned, can, laying everything else aside, once more meet, forgeting, as it were, past differences, on common ground and feel that now mutual interest and sympathy exist, however far assunder they may have been before. How pleasant, how joyful will that time be. Many are anxiously awaiting the period of complete restoration of fraternal feeling. Then will the past be left forever at rest and then will harmony and goodwill once more abound.

What valid reason can be assigned for keeping up this evil spirit, for all the issues involved have long since been settled? If we expect and desire the nation to prosper we must all work heartily together for its upbuilding, and then success will crown our efforts. The passions of excited persons may lead them into great wrong, but a time will come for sound judgment to assert its sway, and then matters are viewed in a different light from what they were before.

During the late war when opposing armies covered the plain and the dull sound of cannon could be heard in Frederick, even from the battle-field at Gettysburg, it is not to be wondered at that excitement ran high, for momentous issues were indeed involved. Mrs. Fritchie amid it all was calm and collected.

"What I do thou knowest not now, but shalt know hereafter," saith Jehovah, and our aged friend believed it fully. We one day shall know that what God has done for you, for me, for all, is undoubtedly the best. And yet this is so hard to learn and understand because we want our own way, and are not willing to be lead by "infinite wisdom." Mrs. Fritchie believed that God saw that it was best for all the people of this great nation to be free and thus make our Declaration of Independence not a mockery, but true and complete. Free as the air we breathe, yes, free as all would wish to be, for who that has enjoyed liberty, for only a single moment, or day, would wish to be bound in chains again. The union of the States must be held inviolate, must not be disturbed. In it there is strength, there is power. We will be held responsible and will unquestionably have to give account for the influence we have exerted. This free, united country, is yet to do a great work in the evangelization of the world. Who can for a moment doubt, but that the "Star Spangled Banner" will eventually be planted in distant lands where darkness and superstition now reign supreme. Glorious Banner, each star and stripe has been baptized in blood, destined

to float, as we believe, from every pinnacle
and dome the wide world over, and proving the harbinger of every blessing. May
we not hope that the day is not distant
when all nations shall enjoy the blessings so
long vouchsafed to us. Columbia, thou hast
given birth to many of the most distinguished
men that have ever lived. Among that number stands the noble Washington, who, at the
close of his term of service as President of the
United States, when he might have pro-
claimed himself, or been declared Emperor
by the people, quietly laid aside the insignia
of office and became a private citizen. What
a noble course was this pursued by the beloved
Father of his country. Civil and religious
liberty has been fully established in the United
States, to continue, we hope, as long as the
world shall stand. We would not interfere
with the powers that be, but we do believe that
ere many years shall have rolled around ty-
rants and despots will learn that their reign
must cease. When we think of Sixteen Hundred and Twenty, when this land was a wilder-
ness, inhabited by savages and wild beasts,
how dismal and gloomy was the scene presented. It was enough to cause the heart to
sink in the strongest man, surrounded, almost,
by the deep, dark ocean, away from friends

and relatives, the passengers and crew of the
"May Flower," all landed, save one, on
Plymouth's rock-bound shore. We cannot
feel too grateful to God for having spared
the lives of those worthy, fearless persons
amid so much privation and danger. Kind
reader, have you ever felt what it is to be
on land or sea in this world and feel that
you are alone. If you have not, would
that you may never experience it. And now,
as these people had left their friends,
never again in all probability to meet with
them in this world, you can readily imagine
what distress and sorrow must have filled their
minds, and yet, for conscience sake, they were
willing to give up all, to forsake all. A funeral at sea! have you ever read of or witnessed
one? If you have I need not remind you of
its solemnity. During the long and tedious
sailing on the restless ocean, but one death
occurred, only one was prevented by Divine
Providence from reaching this country alive.
One was also born on the wild ocean's breast,
Peregrine White, and he landed with the rest.
Sweet babe, the ocean bed was thy cradle, and
the surging of the wild waves the first sound
that thou dids't hear. From that small beginning we are now a great and prosperous
Nation.

What a remarkable example of God's fostering care does this land present. We now number over sixty million souls. When we think of it we are astonished beyond measure, the increase has been so great and rapid. We have in this country every kind of soil and almost every kind of plant, animal and insect, and the variations of climate make it pleasant and agreeable to all. Surely, of a land to which so much is given, much will be required. Let us then be actively engaged in sending forth to the world everything that tends to elevate and benefit mankind. It is very pleasant after traveling on the ocean for a number of days, to see at length the "lighthouse" in the distance. Well, we predict that ere another hundred years shall have passed this country will have become the "Beacon Light" of the world, gleaming forth so that men can see in all directions, making steady advancement in everything calculated to benefit and ennoble the human race, proving the contrary to those who have so sneeringly asserted that a "Republic" cannot endure. A free Church and Ministry, entirely separate from state, is what we must ever approve. We need not fear a foreign foe, for we believe that we are strong enough (even with our poor coast defence) to repel an attempted invasion,

coming from any source whatever. What we
have most to guard against is internal strife
and contention.   No one can help but see that
those countries governed by the liberal principles of God's Word are the countries that are
making the greatest progress in all that tends
to elevate and refine, as well as furnishing the
people with broad and enlightened views.
Christian ladies in this country often take
Bibles and distribute them to the poor and
neglected or sit down and read and explain it
to them.   Doing such work appears as though
Heaven to earth descended. Earth with
Heaven here is blended. It is a glorious
work, such as the Angels might delight to
engage in, taking care of the ignorant and
those possessed of but little of this world's
goods. No where else on earth in religious
matters are individual rights so completely
cared for and protected, and it is surely something that should be highly appreciated. In
this glorious land the poor have equal rights
with the rich, for they have the ballot
placed in their hands and assist in sending
men to Congress whose duty it is to legislate
for the benefit of all their constituents. We
sincerely hope that the day may soon come, or
dawn, when all nations may enjoy the same
blessings that have been granted us for so long

a time, for when the rights of the people are trampled on and not recognized in any way, then is unrest and upheaval. The powerful oppressing the weak and the helpless are crushed to the earth, until at length, the cry goes up to Heaven "Oh Lord how long" may we continue in the enjoyment of peace in this land, and ever move forward and upward in everything that is worthy and commendable, endeavoring to excel in every good word and work, and at length become what the Almighty assuredly designed we should be "the greatest land and people on earth."

My small book must now be brought to a close. In sending it forth I hope that it may be the means of shedding light on some disputed points in the life of my venerable neighbor, and highly esteemed friend, Mrs. Barbara Fritchie. I have stated facts in connection with her four-score years and over, which I hope may prove interesting to all. I have endeavored to impress on the youthful mind the importance of ever showing unswerving devotion to our beloved country. Nothing has been written in haste, or in an unkind, uncharitable spirit, but rather in the true spirit of harmony and love. That it may lead to kindlier and better feelings among those who have long been estranged is my sincere prayer.

I have submitted the manuscript to the nearest relatives of Mrs. Fritchie now living, and after perusal they have stated to me that they believe it to be entirely correct and did not notice anything that should be changed.

 Description of Frederick City.

BEAUTIFUL City of Frederick! Located in the lovely Monocacy valley, between the Catoctin mountain on the West, and the Sugar Loaf mountain on the East, wonder not that we love to stray among thy hills and valleys, for from 1745 when the village of Frederick was located, and named after "Frederick, Prince of Wales," her whole history has been of the most ennobling character. In the early history of this land, when oppressed by the mother country, the sons of Frederick City, and county, went forth with alacrity in her defense and when the demand was again made in 1775 for more soldiers, two companies were

formed, and under command of Captain
Michael Cresop and Captain Thomas Price,
with John Ross Key as subordinate officer,
(Father of Francis Scott Key) marched from
Frederick Town to the camp at Boston to join
Col. Washington. All demands ever made
were most cheerfully responded to. The following highly important utterances were made
by Fredericktown June 17, 1776: "That what
may be recommended by a majority of the
Congress, equally delegated by the people of
the United Colonies we will at the hazard of
our lives and fortune support and maintain;
and that every resolution of the convention
tending to separate this providence from a majority of the Colonies, without the consent of
the people, is destruction to our internal safety
and big with public ruin." On the 17th of
January, 1781, Gen. Morgan won a glorious
victory over Tarleton at the Cowpens. It was
in the pursuit that followed this battle that the
gallant Sargent Everhart, of Frederick county,
saved the life of Col. afterward Gen. George
Washington, at the head of the Virginia cavalry. Many years after when Gen. Washington visited Frederick, he sent for his old friend
Everhart, and grasping his hand embraced
him. The meeting is said to have been quite
affecting. Sargeant Everhart was one of the

rescuers also of Lafayette from his dangerous
situation on the Brandywine. He died in his
86th year within a few miles of Frederick.
We were shown his sword, as well as other
military articles that belonged to him whilst
living, and had the pleasure of seeing him before his death.

In the year 1777 barracks for the garrison
of two battallions of infantey were erected in
Frederick. The old buildings stood long
upon the Southern suburbs of the town, and
have now partially disappeared. The Deaf and
Dumb Asylum stands on the site. They were
used also to confine British prisoners of war.
The old original log jail was also used for the
same purpose. Afterward the barracks was
used by the State of Maryland as an Armory,
and the last use made of the buildings (prior to
the Asylum taking charge of them,) was when
the "Home Guards" of Frederick were guarding the City. The members would meet there
and be sent in squads to guard the different
sections of the City. They used first to meet
at Coppersmith's Hall, corner of Market and
Church streets, and were commanded by Gen.
John A. Steiner, Captain Alfred Brengle,
Captain Saunders and others at different periods. Here permit me to say that justice has
never been done those men who traversed the

streets of the City of Frederick, night after night with guns on their shoulders, and heavy ones they were, during the perilous times just preceeding the war. We were glad to notice honorable mention made of them by Mr. Chas. W. Miller in his recently published "Directory and Business Guide." The position they occupied was perilous indeed. They were to see that nothing was brought into Frederick during the night intended to be conveyed to Virginia for the benefit of the enemy, and were provided with old, heavy guns to execute orders. One evening it was announced that a splendidly equiped military company was coming from Baltimore to pass over to Virginia. We asked Judge Nelson for instruction in regard to entering the City. We were informed that he stated we should allow them to enter, but not suffer them to tarry over night, but go directly on. In a short time they came and we marched them through the City to the suburbs, where, at the "Old Stone Tavern" they asked to get some refreshments, which was granted. We then marched them out to, and about half a mile down the Manor Lane, leading on to the Point of Rocks, when about to separate many of us thought a desperate struggle would ensue, as they were fully prepared and we had nothing but our old guns. We quickly fixed bayonets, depending more on this use of our guns than in fireing for in that mode with their modern arms they had the decided advantage. It being nine or ten o'clock at night and somewhat dark they could not see well how poorly we were prepared to meet them. To our great surprise instead of turning on us and fireing, they gave three hearty cheers to the Home Guards of Frederick.

On Prospect Hill, a short distance beyond where we turn into the Manor Lane, Col. Wm. P. Maulsby, now of Westminster, resided, and as we emerged from the lane that night, the Col. was waiting on horseback and invited us all up to his mansion, where tables ladened with every kind of refreshments were spread, and his estimable wife and daughter did all in their power to make all spend a sociable and pleasant time. When Gov. Hicks was in Frederick, the Home Guards were marching around where he was guarding the hotel the entire night. These are only a few of the incidents that occured during the time they served. Often those who were not on guard lay on the floor of the old barracks all night, without covering. They were presented by the ladies of Frederick with a splendid stand of colors. Hon. Reverdy Johnson, of Baltimore, made the presentation speech in the Court House yard.

We could give the names of those who were young men long ago, and went forth from Frederick in the Revolutionary war to battle for our common country, and came back, after enduring almost superhuman suffering, ruined in health, mere wrecks, having been as far North as Canada, and resting at night without shelter, yet they gladly endured it all for our glorious country. In the war of 1812 Frederick, including the county, again organized artillery and infantry companies and sent them speedily to the front, and in the late war of the Rebellion she sent forth many noble men to battle for the Union and hundreds yeilded up their lives in its defense. With sorrow we state that some of her sons on account of geographical location and family relationship, went into the Southern army.

Frederick was settle to a great extent by emigrants from Germany, and they proved to be hardy, industrious, christian people. They soon erected churches and school houses. The German language was spoken generally throughout the village, and the religious services in the churches were conducted in the same language. But the English as well as the German was taught in the day schools. One of the churches built, when Frederick could scarcely be called a town, yet stands,

although built in the year 1763. It is the old
German Reformed Church. True it was
changed in the interior a few years since to
adapt it to Sunday School purposes, but ex-
ternally it has undergone but little change.
Its noble, lofty spire still points heavenward
as in the days of yore, and the Town Clock in
the steeple still announces to the inhabitants
that time is rolling on. Many years ago, one
Sabbath afternoon during a severe thunder
storm, the steeple was struck by lightning but
not seriously impaired. The English members
of the German Reformed sect in the year
1848 built on the opposite side of the street
one of the most comfortable and beautiful
churches in the State of Maryland. The old
Evangelical Lutheran Church was partially
removed some years ago and a very handsome
and imposing new church, Gothic in style,
erected in front of where the old church stood.
The bells in the belfry of this church are
peculiarly sweet and plaintive in tone. We
have traveled considerably, but never heard
any others of exactly the same sound. They
were, I believe, cast in England, and have considerable silver in the composition. We have
also a very costly Episcopal Church, the old
original church in the Queen Anne style of
architecture being used as a lecture room. The

Methodist Episcopal congregation have also a fine new church; the original church of Methodism was torn down in the Summer of 1886 and now private residences occupy the site.   We have beside a very neat and pretty Presbyterian Church.   St. John's   Roman Catholic Church is large and massive, finished in imitation of granite and having in the steeple a chime ot bells of as sweet tone as found anywhere; also Trinity Chapel, a second Methodist Episcopal Church; a new brick church built by the United Brethen, and a new, very substantial looking church, built by the German Baptists.   The Salvation Army have built a large frame church or barracks at the corner of Fourth and Bentz streets.   The colored people have two large brick churches, and large congregations.   The bells of the several churches we have named have called thousands together to worship in earthly sanctuaries, who are doubtless now singing Jehovah's praise around His throne in glory. The Court House is a very large and conveniently arranged brick building, located in a square surrounded by a grove of forest trees. The old, ancient looking Court House that occupied formerly the site of the present building, was a number of years since destroyed by fire.   Here on the 28th of November, 1765,

the first judical decision was given against the
constitutionality of the "Stamp Act." The Jail
is a new and beautiful brick building, and
stands where a few years since the old Jail
stood, with its heavy iron barred windows and
thick stone walls. Prior to the erection of the
last building we had to depend for the security
of prisoners on an old log Jail. The City Hall
and Market House combined, are well worthy
of notice. The lower, or first story, is where
the "Market" is held, and on a pretty Summer morning a stranger would be surprised to
see the long line of wagons drawn up in front,
and the large amount of every kind of produce
brought in from the rich surrounding county.
The upper portion is used for the Mayor's
office. A large room is nicely fitted up for
this purpose, and back of it is a magnificient
Hall, used for opera purposes, also for political and social meetings. The old Market
House, which stood where the new one now
stands, was built in the year 1769. We have
a number of volunteer Fire Companies, with
elegant steam engines, and everything required to do efficient work. We have a Young
Men's Bible Society, actively engaged in dis-
tributing God's Word, Young Men's Christian
Associations, a Women's Christian Temperance Union, Good Templars, Temple of

Honor, two lodges of Free Masons, the order of Odd Fellows, Knights of Pythias, tribe of Red Men, Knights of Honor, two white and one colored army posts, two brass bands, the Frederick City Cornet, which has acquired great reputation for discoursing splendid music, and Jenkins' Colored Cornet Band, which has been in existence for many years. We can boast of a number of well conducted hotels, the larger of them being the City Hotel, Carlin House, Groff's Hotel, and the New Central. The Frederick Female Seminary is well worthy of notice. It is now considered one of the leading Female Seminaries of the land. It is built in the Corinthian style of Architecture, and is really beautiful, and has for its principal a most worthy christian gentleman, of the highest intellectual culture. The Deaf and Dumb Asylum, built by the State of Maryland, was commenced in the year 1871 and is located here, and has a large attendance of scholars from all parts of the State. Its principal, Prof. Charles W. Ely, is a most estimable gentleman, and thoroughly qualified in every respect for the position. It occupies the most commanding site in the city. From the cupola you have a view of the county in every direction for a considerable distance. Its style of architecture is in the

main Gothic, and wins the admiration of all
beholders. We have also several Orphan
Asylums, and a short distance from the city is
Montevue Hospital; as fine a building as can
be found anywhere for relieving and caring for
the aged, the poor, the distressed. It is heated
by steam and all the food furnished the in-
mates is such as any reasonable person might
feel thankful to partake of. Some years back,
1869, Mr. Louis McMurray, a capitalist, came
here from Baltimore City and established
without asking the citizens to take stock, or
aid him in any way, a corn canning establishment. He has gone on from year to year
putting up new buildings and increasing his
facilities, until it has proven to be a complete
success, showing what enterprise and capital
can do. It is now one of the largest houses
engaged in the business in the United States.
In the regular canning season he gives em-
ployment to eleven hundred hands, and puts up,
or fills as many sometimes as 150 thousand
cans in a single day. Four or five years since
a novelty manufacturing establishment was
started here with home capital, and it appears
to be successful. They have been turning out first-class step ladders and furnishing
a splendid quality of black ink, for which they
have orders from distant sections of the Union.

A hosiery factory has recently been started in our midst by our citizens, and thus far it appears as though it would prove quite a success. We have a number of public and private schools in the city, also the Frederick City College, where, under able professors, a good solid education can be obtained, and where many men who have taken high rank in literature and business circles were taught. The Novitiate of the Catholic Church is an immense educational institution where students are in attendance from all sections of the Union. Though Frederick does not cover much more territory than some years ago, yet it has been greatly improved by tearing down old buildings and placing in their stead new and elegant private residences. The business men have built many splendid store rooms, and each of our banking institutions now transact their business in new and beautiful buildings. How different is this from over a hundred years ago, 1745, when the town of Frederick was laid out by an Englishman, and afterward settled for the most part by worthy, industrious Germans. Then the streets were covered with rows of wooden buildings, scarcely a brick building to be seen. We have several planing factories employing a number of hands; several furniture establishments con-

ducted on an extensive scale, and two founder-
ies; three factories where fertilizers are prepared to a large amount. We also have
within our corporate limits a steam flour mill,
where the very best flour is manufactured in
large quantities, also the City flour mill, oper-
ated in the old way, located on Carroll Creek,
where excellent flour is made and furnished
our citizens; several tanneries, where the best
of leather is manufactured, and a number of
establishments particularly along the banks
of Carroll Creek, where skins are dressed and
gloves are made for wholesale and retail trade;
some four or five coal yards, where every kind
of coal is furnished, and we have several brick
yards, where large quantities of brick are an-
nually made and sold; also several extensive
Coach factories, where the very best carriages
of every kind are manufactured. A large
number of useful and important inventions
have emenated from citizens of Frederick, and
in art we have artists of great ability, who
fully deserve the recognition they have received. Frederick City is supplied with
the very best and purest water brought from
the neighboring mountains and we do
not hesitate to state that purer water can
not be found in this or any other land.
The scenery surrounding Frederick is of

unsurpassed beauty, and is thus acknowledged to be by all unprejudiced persons. We
have great wealth, and yet it is for the greater
part in the hands of those advanced in years
who have sufficient and do not care to embark
in any enterprise however meritorious, hence
our city in all these years has only grown
from a village to a city of about ten thousand
inhabitants. If Northern men of wealth and
influence would settle among us, how different
it would be. Why just think, within five
miles of Frederick we have one of the loveliest
points known to mortal man. It is White
Rock, from the summit of which you have as
lovely a view as is possible for the eye of man
to rest upon, extending into Pennsylvania and
Virginia, with springs of pure, ice cold water
near, also springs strongly impregnated with
iron and sulphur in the immediate vicinity.
It could easily be made a delightful Summer
resort, and yet nothing has been done to make
it such to the present day. We have several
railroads entering the city, making it quite
easy of access and furnishing coal and lumber
at reasonable rates. It was originally intended
that the Baltimore and Ohio Railroad on its
course westward should pass directly through
Frederick, but on account of the treachery of
certain parties wielding considerable influence

this purpose was frustrated, and three miles east of Frederick at Monocacy Junction its course was changed and a branch only extended to our town. The city of Frederick is not laid off as regularly, and the streets are not as straight as you will find in many other cities; particularly is this the case with Patrick street, which would be the prettiest street in the city, were it not for a considerable bend near the centre, which it is now too late to remedy. It is accounted for from the fact, that when the village was first located the National pike leading westward ran in this direction, and the surveying apparatus was crude, and imperfect, hence the result. Carroll Creek, a stream ordinarily low, but after heavy continuous rains rising to a considerable height, passes through the city, running eastward in its course until it reaches the Monocacy. It is spanned by seven iron bridges in its course through the city, entirely supplanting the former old unsightly wooden structures. We have moreover a beautiful cemetery, Mount Olivet. It is a precious place to visit, for here repose not only the remains of our friends and relatives, but many of Frederick's oldest and most respected citizens. Our city is remarkably healthy, as the health officers record will at any time show that the percentage of mortality is less according to the population than in most cities in the Union. We must acknowledge, however, that Frederick notwithstanding its many natural advantages, beauty of location and magnificent scenery, is not yet noted in business circles for energy and advancement and has not increased in population commensurate with the many advantages enjoyed. The Press of the city, consisting of five weekly and two daily papers, is ably conducted. The ability displayed in the editorials, the general selection and arrangement, would do full credit to any city. By means of telegraph and telephones in our midst we are enabled to communicate with all points with the greatest ease. Although Frederick has not increased so rapidly in population, it is and always will be a city of considerable importance, for it is surrounded by a county of the greatest fertility, producing almost every kind of grain and fruit and her agriculturists are men of enlarged views and highly intelligent farmers, which is abundantly shown by adopting the latest and most approved agricultural implements and by the annual displays at our Fair, held at the beautiful grounds of the Society, on the suburbs of the city, where fine buildings have been constructed and where almost everthing that nature or art has ever produced is on exhibition.

Not desiring to be two lengthy or by any means tedious, I will now bring my description to a close.

THE END.

www.ingramcontent.com/pod-product-compliance
Lightning Source LLC
Chambersburg PA
CBHW030017030726
47499CB00008B/3035